CW00662124

HADDO REIMAGINED

HADDO REIMAGINED

Stories Inspired by Photographs of Haddo Country Park

RAE COWIE AND SUSAN ORR

Kelly Pearl Publishing

Eryngium Giganteum

Contents

DEDICATION   ix

INTRODUCTION

INSPIRED BY LANDMARKS AT HADDO

1   FILLING THE EMPTY FRAME   6

2   KEMBLE'S SEAT   12

3   BRICK BY BRICK   16

4   EVEN THE DEAD CAN BE HAUNTED BY AN URN   22

5   MILESTONES   28

6   CANARY ON THE TENNIS COURT   32

INSPIRED BY NATURE AT HADDO

7   BUTTERBUR   38

8   THE LIGHTEST TOUCH LEAVES A BRUISE   44

9   WE COULD NEVER FIND A BETTER HOME THAN HADDO   48

INSPIRED BY VISITORS TO HADDO

10 FOLLOW IN THE FOOTSTEPS OF ...   56

ACKNOWLEDGEMENTS   59
BIOGRAPHIES   64
GLOSSARY OF DORIC TERMS   67

First published 2024
By Kelly Pearl Publishing,
Contact kellypearlpublishing@gmail.com

ISBN: 978-1-7384699-0-1

Text copyright © Rae Cowie 2024

All photography except on the page listed below is copyright © Susan Orr 2024
Page 16 Vivien Gauld

The right of Rae Cowie and Susan Orr to be identified as the author and photographer of this work has been asserted by them in accordance with the Copyright, Designs and Patents Act 1988.

All rights reserved. No part of this publication may be reproduced, stored in a retrieval system, or transmitted in any form, or by any means, mechanical, photocopying, recording or otherwise, without permission in writing from the publisher.

This story collection is entirely a work of fiction. The names, characters and incidents portrayed in it, whilst at times based on historical figures, are the work of the author's imagination.

Every effort has been made to trace copyright holders and obtain their permission for the use of copyright material. The publisher apologises for any errors or omissions and would be grateful if notified of any corrections that should be incorporated in future reprints or editions of this book.

A CIP catalogue record for this title is available from the British Library.

With love to Mum and Dad, Isobel and Ian Addison,
who first took me on walks around
Scotland's beautiful countryside.
- Rae

For Gordon, James & Adam,
whose love and encouragement continually
inspire my photographic journey.
- Susan

Discover the inspiration behind **Haddo Reimagined**, located around Aberdeenshire's Haddo Country Park at places indicated by the key.

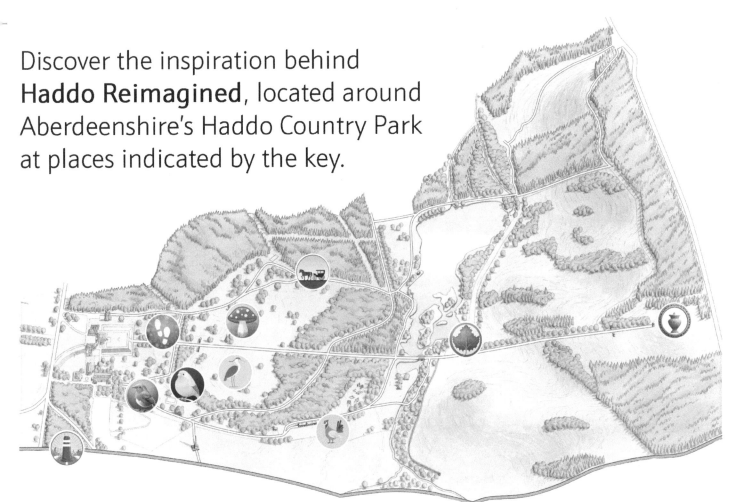

Inspired by Landmarks at Haddo

Filling the Empty Frame

Sensory Garden

Kemble's Seat

Kemble's Seat

Brick by Brick

Pheasantry

Even the Dead can be Haunted by an Urn

Giant Urn

Milestones

On the driveway leading into Haddo

Canary on the Tennis Court

Tennis Courts

Inspired by Nature at Haddo

Butterbur

By the bridge over the Lake

The lightest touch leaves a bruise

A wildlife tree in the Doolies area

We could never find a better home than Haddo

Doolies area, south of the Scots Mile near the Balustrade

Inspired by Visitors to Haddo

Follow in the footsteps of...

Tree lined avenue leading to formal gardens and house

Autumn Fern

INTRODUCTION

Over a finger-numbing crisp autumn, photographer Susan Orr explored the picturesque pine forests and meadows of Haddo Country Park, discovering extraordinary tales about fungi and fairies, ghostly sightings and Stone-Age settlements, herbal medicine and the importance of herons.

In the cool damp by the bubbling burn, she spied nodding purple pincushions of devil's-bit scabious. A pretty flower whose Latin name means to scratch, it was traditionally used to treat scabies and sores. Its stubby roots appear bitten, legend has it, after the Devil grew furious at the plant's soothing properties and tried to destroy it.

In springtime, swathes of Haddo are carpeted with delicate harebells, known in Scotland as bluebells, and in olden times as witches' bells or old man's bells (the 'old man' being the Devil).

Susan shared her initial storyboard of photographs with writer Rae Cowie, who became entranced by the beauty, enormous variety, and medicinal importance of Haddo's botanical heritage.

This led Rae to research accounts of local women accused of witchcraft, and the case of Marioun Grant, said to have the Devil's mark branded on her wrist. Found guilty of charming swords to protect their owners from harm, the poor soul confessed to learning healing skills from Christonday (the Devil). Executed in April 1597, she inspired Rae's story *Butterbur*.

As spiders spun webs between fern fronds, and mist curled over the lake, Susan and Rae drank coffee and ate scones (much of the project was fuelled by coffee and scones) as they considered which of Haddo's many mysteries and secrets to share in a book.

One legend that instantly made the cut was the prophecy of the 13th-century seer Thomas the Rhymer.

When the heron leaves the tree,
The Laird o' Gight will landless be.

In 1787, shortly before the sale of neighbouring Gight Castle and its lands by Catherine Gordon (mother of the Romantic poet, Lord Byron) to George Gordon of Haddo, a siege of herons, who'd lived at Gight for many years, flew from the grounds, never to return. Despite Rhymer's warning, George Gordon continued to ride the five miles between Haddo and Gight, and in 1791, on a perfect summer's day, was thrown from his horse and died.

The new Lord Haddo quickly abandoned the cursed estate of Gight, which soon fell into disrepair – *The Laird o' Gight will landless be* – fulfilling the soothsayer's prediction.

This cautionary tale, and the importance of herons continuing to nest at Haddo, sparked Rae's new fairy tale *We Could Never Find a Better Home Than Haddo*.

As Susan hauled her bags and tripod, waiting for the perfect light to capture Haddo's landmarks, Rae became riveted by the story behind a 20-foot-high granite urn. Mounted on a grand pedestal, on a hill overlooking the woods, it dominates the vista. Erected in 1848 by George Hamilton-Gordon, 4th Earl of Aberdeen (prime minister 1852–1855), it commemorates his beloved first wife, Lady Catherine Hamilton, and their three daughters, who died young of tuberculosis.

Despite continuing to wear mourning dress for the rest of his life, three years after the loss of Lady Catherine, he remarried, but the union with Harriet Douglas was an unhappy one and, sadly, she too died young, at 41. It struck Rae as heartbreaking that, despite Harriet bearing the earl five children, Haddo has no monument to her memory. Determined that she should not be forgotten, Rae has given Harriet's ghost a voice in *Even the Dead Can Be Haunted by An Urn*.

So, if you are a regular guest of Haddo Country Park, or have yet to visit, or simply wish to meditate awhile with photographs and stories inspired by a remarkable place, please sit back and allow Haddo to work its magic.

Rae Cowie and Susan Orr
SEPTEMBER 2024

INSPIRED BY LANDMARKS
AT HADDO

I

FILLING THE EMPTY FRAME

Not that long ago, Eleanor had loved to stride to the top of the hill with long views back to the house, but her hip troubled her now, and she was pleased to make it as far as the sensory garden. Midweek during term time suited her best, when she mostly had the place to herself, kept company by the trickle of pond water and the chirp of a skinny robin.

Today though, no sooner had she settled on the bench, when a ruddy-cheeked lad rushed in, followed by a woman shoving a pram whilst dragging an empty scooter. The boy shrieked and scampered around the willow maze before thumping on the pump that spluttered then gushed with pond water.

The robin rose to the safety of a bare branch, which wobbled under him.

The child stood on tiptoe to peer through the spyhole of a giant rusted camera, something even adults liked to do. When he grew bored, his mum lifted him to feel the velvety softness of Lamb's Lugs, to rub rosemary stems between his fingers and smell.

Her baby whimpered.

'Would you mind if we joined you?' The young mum was pale. 'I'd hoped we'd make the play area before she needed a feed.'

'Take a seat,' Eleanor said.

The woman unzipped her thick coat and set the baby to her breast then tore open a packet of crisps and handed them to the boy. The robin flew down to peck at fallen crumbs, making the child squeal. But the pieces were large, and Eleanor worried too much salt might harm the bird. She stuck out her trainer and toed the titbits beneath the bench.

'What do you like best?' she asked the boy, thinking he might say the water pump or maze.

Instead, he pointed to an enormous picture frame, large enough to be a panto prop, which stood in the opposite corner.

'Would you mind taking our photo ... when we're done?' the mum asked. 'Their dad works offshore.'

'Of course.' Eleanor smiled.

Eleanor and the robin had seen it all.

Children who sang *cheese*, their mouths stretched wide. Chattering school groups. Giggling Brownies. Grandparents holding grandchildren high. Dog owners who crouched beside curly cockapoos, Dalmatians, lively spaniels. She remembered a pretty Labrador who posed, paws crossed. Occasionally, even a sullen teen pouted for a selfie.

Once the baby was fed and the boy's crisps gone, Eleanor snapped the family's picture before they moved on. Quiet settled again. The robin landed near the bench and cocked his head. Eleanor took the bag of birdfeed she had bought at the café and dropped fingerfuls onto the path like Hansel, or was it Gretel who laid a trail through the woods?

The robin ran then stopped. Ran then stopped.

His spindly legs appeared barely thick enough to steady him. She spoke softly, warning him of the icy weather to come that would make her hip ache. Bob, bob, bob, he pecked at the seeds. She sprinkled a route until he sat, tiny, in the centre of the wooden frame. Then she sidestepped, slowly, joining him.

2

KEMBLE'S SEAT

Extract from a letter written 10 July 1817 by actor, John Philip Kemble to his darling sister, Sarah Siddons …

The bone-rattling journey by carriage from London to Haddo is not for the faint-hearted, and particularly troublesome for one who is tall. I cannot deny that the regular need to stop for fresh horses and coachman was most welcome. Still, I find it curious when well-meaning friends and patrons, some who have travelled no further than the next county, enquire whether Edinburgh might be far enough. As if northern Scotland swarms with savages and there is nothing of artistic interest north of the Forth.

None, I would wager, have visited Haddo. For if they had, they would know that the hunting of fallow deer is as marvellous as any in the whole of England, and that, of an evening, guests dance a most excellent quadrille. Why, there are rumours the Bard himself visited Aberdeen, with a group of players who performed *Twelfth Night*. How glorious it must have been. It saddens me that, nowadays, the great playwright's work must be sanitised for the delicate disposition of ladies, whilst intemperance fuels parlour gossip.

Let them chatter like sparrows in the hedgerows about my sojourns north, for they are ignorant that my venerable friend, the 4th Earl, keeps some rather fine wine. I brush aside impertinent questioning about my love of this place, with vague notions of requiring space and time.

For how can I explain that an actor must breathe? That it is frustrating for one with a reputation for playing the gothic to be dragooned into directing amateur house party theatricals, with the focus firmly on wit; that the winter fogs of the city are difficult for an asthmatic; that lavish furnishings soften the brain.

Here, the air is crisp in the lungs, and I have no need to cough, or set aside time for endless rounds of whist. Tramping pleasant woodland helps ease my damned gout. I rehearse; my audience, a flutter of inquisitive crows, who peck amongst rustling leaves at the prickly casings of beechnuts.

How I envy birds their simplistic life. No need to consider the installation of gas lighting in a theatre, or how it must alter the way productions will be staged. Or, most importantly, how the devil such costs must be funded! All worries that remain firmly in the city.

Little wonder then, that even when the sharp rain of Haddo spits angry against my cheeks, and the boulder I sit on digs hard into my spine, I remain adamant that there is no finer chair for contemplation than this seat of mossy stone.

Your loving brother,
J. P. Kemble

3

BRICK BY BRICK

1843 - PHEASANTRY

'Pit them there, Walter.' Davy pointed to a bourach of reid bricks.

'Fit a tyauve ... Aa for cooshie doos!' There wis a clink as Walter drappit the load.

'Oors is nae to ask, Walter ... Only the best for her ladyship.' Fan he saa the drawings, Davy had nearly fainted clean awa. It was the size o it. A *palace* for phasies and chooks to sharn, wi doos in the reef.

'Fit wye are they gan to aa this bather, biggin summin si fantoosh?' Walter scrappit his nib.

Davy was a freen o his faither and kent the loon needed work, but sometimes he wunnert if Walter had a neep for a heid. Davy cleared his thrapple.

'Do you ging to the kirk?'

'Ay ... maist Sundays ... unless Dad needs a han with the hairst.' Walter blushed and looked at his beets.

'Weel, you'll have heard o the last supper. Even phasies deserve a decent send aff.'

Davy had seen birds daunderin like his lordship, nae kennin they wid flee, wild-eened, as they skiffed ower hedges. Only to be shot and flung in a pile, like a bourach o bricks.

Permission granted by Vivien Gauld

1920 – HAMES

Fa would have thocht it? Biden in the poultry yards! But it took mair than a firie in the grate to turn the place into a hame. Robina kent she should be fair trickit wi dryin ropes and a muckle gairden wi a tattieboodie, far Alex grew lang dreels o leeks an peas. They'd even their ain lavvie oot the back.

But for months noo, they'd pecked at ane anither, baith feart to mention that there wis nae sign o a chookie. Althou, her gweed-mither wis aye quick to claik, saying Robina wis lookin gey peelie-wally.

She took oot a bowl and girdle and baked bannocks for Alex's piece. The warm smell aye won him roun. She piled a pucklie, in a mound, ablow a dry cloot.

PRESENT DAY – RESTROOMS

Each week, Kirsten pushed the buggy around the pond, as Brodie pointed at swans, until they came to the clutch of ducks where she stopped, and he threw fat fistfuls of seed. Today though, her son sat red-cheeked, wailing. He'd been awake most of the night, teething. Friends reminded her maternity leave flew by. Was it wrong to count the days until she returned to the drawing office?

'Let's get you sorted,' she said.

Brodie howled.

The buggy bounced over dried pine needles and roots, along the woodland trail, past the new zip wire and climbing frame, towards the toilet block which sat rust-coloured and handsome as the pheasants it once housed. Its brickwork shone, intricate and precise as a bird's wing. The repurposing of old buildings fascinated her.

The rocking of the buggy had quietened Brodie and he stared at a weathervane that spun in the winter sunshine.

'A cockerel,' she said, as she lifted him from the blankets then shoved on the toilet door, relieved when it opened.

Inside, she laid him on a changing mat and removed his shoes and socks, his fleecy jacket and trousers, before stacking them in a wee pile.

'Almost done, son.' She wiped him clean.

Kirsten knew the structure once housed families, probably busy with mams who browned mince and boiled tatties, steeped nappies to hang on the line. Stirred cream into porridge, darned socks, scrubbed faces as well as linoleum. Did those women drink tea and cry?

Instagram shared endless reels of super-cute #toddlerlife. No one posted photos of runny noses or chins red raw with dribbling – the hard slog of parenting hidden from the click of the camera.

But maybe things weren't so different for the mams of bygone days. Kirsten recently read extracts from the *Onward and Upward* magazine, established by Lady Ishbel Aberdeen, for the *material, mental and moral elevation of women.* Although most of the advice was outdated, a section stuck in her mind; *Every mother has dark days – when the little voices sound shrill and piercing, and little tempers are unruly ... generally speaking, this is the result of the mother's physical weariness and, if possible, she should rest.*

Kirsten bundled Brodie back into his things and picked him up, smiling as he snuggled his shining cheek into the crook of her neck.

Outside, she set him into the buggy and as she strolled past the Palladian mansion, his eyelids drifted shut. So, she swung by Mrs Smith's café and treated herself to a latte, with a thick slice of Biscoff rocky road.

4

EVEN THE DEAD CAN BE HAUNTED
BY AN URN

The monkey puzzle specimen was shipped from Chile, surviving the storms of Cape Horn, to finally dock amongst the damp grass of Haddo. We were lucky it appeared to enjoy the spot and has grown taller than any man. How unsettled it must have felt to be uprooted then planted in a strange, cold land. Perhaps that is why I was drawn to it so.

My marriage to George was difficult from its beginnings. Why, even though he knew I was *enchanted* by the story of the seedling transported halfway around the globe, he insisted the monkey puzzle be planted near the top of the hill. So I strode there daily, to watch over its slow growth and to enjoy the open aspect of deer grazing in the park.

But now George has erected an Urn on the crest of the hill — blighting the view.

The blessed Urn!

A grand, granite sculpture of a jar set upon a sturdy plinth. A magnificent monument, constantly visible when promenading the lawns, or following pretty Candlemas bells along paths in the woods. It looms in plain sight of the drawing room, observable even from the bedchambers.

It's a loving memorial to George's first wife, the adored Catherine Hamilton-Gordon, Countess of Aberdeen, taken too soon by consumption. Not that I — Harriet, the mere second wife — dared utter a complaint about the shadow she cast upon my marriage. It would have appeared indelicate for a lady to protest.

But when George indulged in too much brandy after dinner, I was awoken by him laughing in the moonlight, his countenance flushed with happiness. When I gently touched his arm, he brushed my fingers aside, wishing only to be with *her* as she wandered our rooms.

By morning, his expression hung melancholic again.

I suffered the most ghoulish nightmares, in which Catherine lay pale and slumped by our bedside. Staring. Often, as I fulfilled my wifely duty, I felt certain he moaned for her.

And *her* stiff dead, a decade and more.

A dark cravat and black-bordered handkerchief were his constant companions. There was nothing light about his demeanour to suggest he was brimming with fresh love. And yet I – as a widow, also well acquainted with the agonising pain of grief – upon remarriage, continued to smile! We should have been united by sad circumstance, but George would not permit it.

It is said that speaking whilst in the presence of a monkey puzzle brings bad luck, and this family has endured enough. So, I cross the brow of the hill. Above, the Urn towers, dark against the bone white of the afternoon sky. Beneath my glove, the plinth is icy to touch.

'Where is *my* Urn?' I whisper, urgent as a breeze through the trees.

It's not as if George's finances are troubled. There are rumours of him making prime minister.

'I was faithful ... bore him five children ... Four lusty sons who played leapfrog, grew pink-cheeked as they wrestled on the lawns. Yet, not one matched the limp stillborn you offered,' I hiss.

The stone stands firm.

'I, too, died young ... We were not so different, you and I.'

But Catherine remains silent. Her dominant presence haunts me, even in death.

Something rustles in the undergrowth. A squirrel? A pheasant? I check the surrounding woodland.

Despite its trials, my monkey puzzle stands straight and broad in the weak winter sunshine. Glossy. Thriving. It reaches out and upwards.

I float the lang Scot's mile back to the house, light with the knowledge that I may not have a chilly Urn erected in my memory, but the tree I diligently attended has rooted and flourishes.

Monkey Puzzle Branch

5

MILESTONES

The last time Logan ran was dressed as Santa, firing on Jägerbombs, fundraising for a music therapy charity. He was lighter then, both in weight and spirit. He pounds past the convenience store, with its tempting offer of a smoked bacon bap with a coffee-to-go, and heads out of town. His playlist beats at just the right tempo, as he crosses the humped-back bridge, where the river burst its banks and swirls across the muddy field. Goosebumps prick his thighs. He could be at home, warm, practising the Jew's harp; a bargain he bought off eBay to keep his mind sharp. Not that he's shown it to Sarah. It's tucked in a battered-leather shaving bag that kicks around the bottom of the wardrobe. If he turned around now, he could practise 'Tonight Will Be Fine', before giving the toilet a damned good clean.

The previous evening, Sarah reminded him that her parents are coming for the weekend and the tin of polish is kept below the stairs. Partner in an accountancy firm, she's probably dealt with her first client of the day. She says she's fine with him taking time out, that it's great to have help with the kids — *as if he never helped before* — and he imagined it'd be a piece of piss, with all day to sort out the house before collecting the girls. But he hates the tone she uses when things aren't kept shipshape, when he nips to the chippy for dinner, when Phoebe's spelling isn't done by the time Sarah dashes through the door.

His breath steams as he finds his stride.

But *she* didn't have to handle the wailing, when Amelie arrived home from school with a chunk missing from her fringe. Turns out safety scissors are a danger. Then Phoebe had a playdate, where she wore a virtual reality headset, but the cliff-edge view made her dizzy and she'd landed face-first on tiling, requiring a dash to A&E and four stitches in her forehead — howling that she wanted Mummy. Logan had wanted Mummy too!

His lungs burn.

Jeez, he never saw it coming. Never imagined he would lose his job. Not even when they turned the temperature down in the swimming pool and kiddies huddled on the side like penguins in a snowstorm.

He bends double. He'd had more energy during the Santa run, even after a heavy night out.

He straightens, heart thumping as he slows to a walk, past staring sheep, until he comes to the shelter of pines, when his watch beeps, a reminder he *really* should go home. He takes a breather beside a narrow, pillared stone with a mossy 18 carved into its side. An ancient thing. A milestone, reminding him how far he's come.

Five miles at most.

He traces his finger around the numbers. What's he done since he was 18?

Left school with a handful of miserable grades. Failed as a musician. Trained as a lifeguard. Fell in love with Sarah. Ran fundraising marathons to impress her. Proposed on Hogmanay as fireworks painted the sky. Become a proud father.

It doesn't feel like much. Maybe if he'd had a dad around to say, *Well done, loon,* things might have turned out differently.

He scrapes stubborn lichen from the numerals with his thumbnail.

On Saturday evenings, when they're all cuddled on the couch, munching popcorn, watching some cheesy movie, he worries it might all be taken away. Until the girls laugh and Sarah smiles, and he squeezes her hand, never wanting to let go.

He'd searched *redundant* in an on-line dictionary and found words like *superfluous, outmoded, unnecessary* – which was shit, because the girls still needed him.

He enjoyed teaching them how to ice-skate, took them long, slow walks to hear seals honk on the beach, was patient with their endless questions. *Does a zebra need a reflective jacket in the dark? Do puffins really puff? Does saying a swear word make you drunk?*

The milestone is weathered, but still standing tall. Maybe he missed other numbers as he ran. He'll look for them on the way home.

Once he's loaded the laundry and scoured the bathroom until it sparkles, he'll look for volunteering work. Something that involves music, for fatherless boys.

6

CANARY ON THE TENNIS COURT

I plant the tripod on the crumbling surface of the tennis court, avoiding weeds that thrust through the cracks. Bats flap as I strive in the dark to attach my camera to the stand. I fumble with the shutter release cable, my fingers stiff with cold.

Beyond the rusted chain-link fence, deep in the woods, an owl screeches.

The big house has its fair share of stories. Floorboards rattling in the attic. Spirits chasing servants through vaulted cellars. Sightings of an apparition named Archie Gordon, who, as a child, kept pet canaries. Poor sod was killed in a motorcar accident. Like Scott.

Scott would have been upset to see me here alone, would have insisted I bring a friend.

'I'm okay,' I say, as if he might hear.

Conditions are perfect for the eclipse. It was Scott who'd been the real photographer. I tagged along sometimes, and he'd taught me about composition and exposure. He'd known when Venus was visible, could pick out the steady red of Mars. I wish I'd listened.

The gate squeaks.

'Hello?' I call.

No answer.

For the hundredth time that day I wish Scott was by my side. I'd crawled into bed, but knew I should be here, in case he showed up to watch. Crazy.

Leaves rustle. It's only the wind.

I lift my flask of steaming lemon tea from my backpack and unscrew the lid. Scott used to make our brew. Except he called it a fly cup, whatever the time of day. It's the little things that swell and choke me. I gulp on the bitter drink.

Somewhere, out in the black, a creature barks.

I tense, mug halfway to my mouth. 'Who's there?' My voice is small in the inky night.

Something hits my chest.

I flinch, scalding my fingers with tea as I blunder backwards.

There's frantic fluttering around my head as the mug drops and I cling to Scott's camera, cowering.

'Please!'

More flapping. I crouch, scared the creature will become entangled in my hair.

The tripod wobbles. I grab at it, but it topples, flinging Scott's precious kit to the ground. I fall to my knees, scrambling amongst nettles, wishing I'd brought a head torch. With stinging fingers, I unplug the cable and brush grit from the lens, feeling a jagged crack. I howl. 'Scott!'

Wings beat. There's sharp twittering.

The moon passes through the Earth's shadow and hangs, peachy plump. Silence.

On the baseline, a man bends and tenderly lifts a palm-sized bundle from the court. He straightens and wails, splitting the air with a cry that would rouse the hounds resting in Haddo's pet cemetery.

I know fierce pain. The kind that cuts you down on a Monday morning, when loading laundry, or making the bed. The kind that bruises your chest and leaves you weak for hours.

I shiver, too afraid to move. Does he expect me to rise and run? To roar?

But the worst has already happened. Losing Scott has numbed me. I clutch his broken camera to my chest.

The stranger steps towards me. He's in hunting tweeds, fresh-faced, mid-twenties at most. His skin is icy blue, his eyes glassy. Tears cling to his lashes, shine on his cheeks. His hands cup a quivering bird. A single yellow feather floats, as if dancing on a string.

The canary forces a chirp, its tiny breast panting. Breaths puff soft as smoke.

I struggle to catch air.

Archie – it must be Archie. The bird grows still. He strokes the canary with his thumb and pulls a silk handkerchief from his breast pocket, wrapping it like a shroud around its body, before placing a light kiss on its head.

'You still *feel*.' I'd imagined Scott hollowed out.

'Of course,' he says.

For months I'd searched for proof of an afterlife, performing rituals clutching amethyst crystals, praying to any god who might listen.

I push to my feet and dust dirt from my jeans.

'They're timid birds,' he says, gazing at the lifeless creature. 'I wanted her to know freedom.'

I imagine a ghostly canary stretching its wings, swooping amongst the conifers.

'I'm sorry.' My voice rings tinny in my ears. I look away, offering him a moment of privacy.

The camera trembles as I return it and the tripod to their cases.

'It's okay, Scott,' I whisper, certain he'll hear. It doesn't matter that I've missed my chance to photograph the heavens.

By the time I've packed everything away, the moon glimmers waxen again and my heart is lighter, but Archie and his canary are gone.

After The Rain

INSPIRED BY NATURE AT HADDO

7

BUTTERBUR

'Look aifter yersel, Quine.' Auld Wilyam nodded.

Quine! Her fingers were as twisted as hazel twigs. Her creaking knees warned of rain.

'I mine on you wi a fine heid o hair, Wilyam, fan we skimmed stanes across the Ythan.'

He slipped a handful of fresh yarrow leaves into his pocket, her remedy for toothache.

'Ay, happy days,' he said.

Maybe it was the pain in his jaw or the sweet smoke from smouldering ling that made his eyes glisten. He clasped her hands too long, then tipped his worn cap and left.

Before Wilyam had snecked the door, Marioun grabbed a rickety stool and stood on it, tugging bunches of dried sneezewort and devil's-bit scabious from the rafters. Her heart skittered quick as a mouse as she gathered butterfly wings, a rabbit's foot, the skull-white feather of a swan, and threw them onto the fire, which crackled and spat. From below her flattened mattress, she retrieved a pouch of birch fungus and tipped its contents into the flames. Pale spores curled black.

No sooner was she done when the pounding of hooves was followed by angry shouts and loud chapping on the door.

'Open up.' The voice was stern. Not a neighbour then.

She took a deep breath.

More rapping. 'We're here for Marioun Grant.'

'Haud your wheesht. I'm comin.'

When she opened the door, a flurry of men crowded in, so many she worried the walls wouldn't hold them. Their cheeks were flushed with the march from the village.

'Are you Marioun Grant?'

'That I am.'

Marioun knew little of the speaker, but the others she knew well. Alex the Flesher — who had been grateful of her attentions when he chopped off his middle finger. Andro the Blacksmith — who cried like a bairn each time she'd salved his burns. Jamesie the Shepherd — who had as many babes as lambs, or so it seemed, and Marioun had helped his poor wife, God rest her soul, to birth each one.

Wilyam ... Even Wilyam was there.

'We're here on the charge of witchcraft,' the baillie said.

Marioun clutched at the table. 'Fit proof div you hae?'

'There have been sightings of a black stag.'

She fingered the edges of her apron. She knew what he meant. The Devil's beast.

'Spik sense. There are nae stags here.' She looked at each of the men she'd aided, who glanced, as one, at their boots.

The baillie's chest puffed. 'Is it true you cure men and beasts with south-running water?'

Marioun's neck prickled.

'An fit o it?' She raised her chin. 'I'm nae witch. A rowan sproots at my door.'

He seized her by the forearm and yanked up the sleeve of her shift.

'See here …' He smirked at the gathering. 'The Devil's mark.'

'Na!' she snorted. 'If she'd aye been here, ma mither wid vouch I was born wi the thing.'

'There's talk you consort with the Queen of Elphame!'

Her guts turned to water.

For months now, rumours had swirled as suspicion pitted neighbour against neighbour.

'Idle claik,' she managed. 'Look aboot, fit div you see but the peer hame o an auld wifie?'

She knew her pleas were in vain, that her fate had been decided. That she would be held in chains, then tried at the Tolbooth, where folk would gaup and roar as the chancellor pronounced her guilty.

The baillie sniffed and glanced at her meagre chattels, the pots and jars she used to mix potions.

'What's that?' He pointed at leaves neatly stacked on the table.

'Butterbur,' she said.

'Picked before sunrise, no doubt.'

'Fan it's at its best.'

She took a limp leaf and handed it to him.

Wilyam coughed. 'She wraps butter in it … wi nae hairm deen.'

The other men shushed him and shoved him towards the door.

The baillie waited for the jostling to settle. He stared.

'What say you in your defence?'

Marioun knew his kind, who crept to her door on moonless nights, seeking unguents for a rash.

He swung a set of manacles. 'If you make no denial, then …'

'I've seen your ain wifie picking butterbur by the burn, to bile the reets,' Marioun said, 'for her sair heids.'

The room fell silent. Not a mote of dust stirred, as fear glimmered in the baillie's eyes.

Butterbur

Devil's-bit scabious

8

THE LIGHTEST TOUCH LEAVES A BRUISE

A ratty squirrel races along a branch, its red tail as fiery as the bumfluff that darkens my chin.

'Kyle, look! It's *so* cute.' Ellie grips my arm as though I might scarper too.

We'd bombed along country roads in her mum's hybrid Polo, taking corners so fast I almost puked.

I squeeze her hand and we duck beneath a fir, deeper into Haddo's woods where it's shady with rhododendrons knotted above our heads. Curled petals carpet the ground.

'Almost there,' I say.

We walk, hunched, until pine needles crunch beneath our trainers, as we pass a rotting conifer felled in a gale. Its flaking bark runs with skittering ants.

'The next one looks better,' I offer.

'You choose the weirdest places,' she says, as we sit on the toppled trunk of an insect-free spruce.

'It's a good place to sketch.'

'I've a better idea,' she says.

She kisses me and I slip my hand beneath her Arctic Monkeys T-shirt. Her skin is warm, her heart thuds beneath my palm.

'Say it,' she breathes, as if she might will words from my mouth.

I pull back a little. Her eyes are rich, like acorns.

I swallow, my throat tight. In movies, it comes out just right.

She yanks my hand from her bra and wriggles out of my arms.

'Why won't you say it?' She shuffles away, undoing her ponytail so her hair swishes, only to grasp it again and twist until it sits coiled at the base of her neck. The spot that's soft and smooth.

Ellie's made it the best summer ever. Picnics of popcorn and cans of cider; cycle rides to an over-grown churchyard where we lie between the headstones; evenings tangled on her duvet listening for her mum's footsteps on the stairs.

'Look at this,' I say, trying to lighten the mood.

To our left, a plate-sized mushroom sprouts from the decaying log. A furrowed brown shelf with a crusted cap, it breaks away easily. I hold it carefully by the sides. Underneath the flesh is pale.

'What is it?' Ellie asks.

'Bear bread.' I smile.

She nudges my shoulder.

'It's called an artist's bracket. Watch.' I pull a toothpick from my pocket. 'We need to hold it gently. The lightest touch leaves a bruise.'

She leans in close, her perfume sweet as forest flowers as I press precisely, carving an E and a K, intricately intertwined. The letters emerge in a delicate shade of cinnamon.

With my mouth dry as a pine cone, I set the artwork gently onto her knees.

'Thank you,' Ellie whispers.

Tears shimmer in her eyes as she reaches and clasps my face, as tenderly as I'd held the mushroom, and we kiss and kiss.

ARTIST'S BRACKET MUSHROOM

Grows wild on stumps
Its cap furrowed, unvarnished
Below, a canvas!

Artist's Bracket Mushroom

9

WE COULD NEVER FIND A BETTER HOME THAN HADDO

Moonlight made frost twinkle, as Damsel picked her fairy feet through the frozen grass. Her pockets were stuffed with ripe rowan berries for Granny, who would be proud of how many she'd picked. But the fruit was heavy and there was no way Damsel could fly home, across the wide meadows called the Doolies. She wasn't afraid of the darkness, now visitors with their big licky-tongued dogs had gone home, but still, Granny had warned her not to dawdle.

She sang her favourite fairy song, over and over, as she went:

Whilst children dream, sprites skip unseen,
Around the gardens, by the lake.
Through golden gates, beside the deer,
Dance fairies to an elfin band.
That plucks and toots and tinkles, loud,
'Til break of day, when field mice sleep.
In Craigie Woods, the berries ripen, full and sweet,
And Oberon sings, blessing Haddo's land.

Soon she came to the pair of tall pine trees that offered shelter in the middle of the meadow. She stopped, her singing voice trapped in her throat.

Up ahead lay a large shadow, a grey hump. It looked like an enormous mole hill. Except it smelt fishy, like the toads who live on the riverbank. Her heart hammered as little puffs of air escaped from the top of an extra-long beak. The pale chest rose in sharp gasps. Its skinny legs lay crumpled underneath it.

It was a heron, from a nest on the other side of the forest.

What if it rose and snatched her? What if it lifted her high as it skimmed across the lake, far, far away and she never saw Granny again?

She should tip the berries from her pockets and take to her wings. But the berries were precious; Granny needed them to make hot rowan juice. She would be upset if Damsel lost them.

Damsel wished she hadn't wasted time singing. Instead, she should have hurried straight to Granny's.

She tiptoed nearer, slowly, trying to edge past, afraid to wake it.

A beady yellow eye blinked open.

Damsel froze.

The heron stared.

Damsel swallowed.

The heron tried to spread his wings, but he was too weak and sank onto the chilly ground with a sad oomph.

'Are you hurt?' she asked.

A shining tear slid along his beak and plopped onto the grass.

She reached out a hand, still afraid to touch him.

'What happened?' Damsel asked.

'When the lake … was … iced … over … I drank from a ditch.' The heron's voice was low.

'What can I do?' she whispered, worried the water must have been bad.

'Do … you … have … a little eel?'

Damsel shuddered. Eels were slithering, snaky creatures that hid in water amongst the rocks. Far too huge for a fairy to catch. Her throat tightened. She'd much rather have sweet things, like wild raspberries, or milk warmed with heather honey.

'I have berries.' She offered a palmful from her pocket.

The heron's head sank.

'No, no. Don't give up,' she said.

She couldn't let him die. She remembered Granny's tale: if the herons left Haddo, then *the land shall lairdless be*, meaning the landowner would leave and nothing would grow and her animal friends would lose their homes. She had to get help! But who?

The night was bitter, and Granny's bad chest meant she must stay indoors by the fire. The Doolies were wide and empty, except for a bouncing deer, who stopped for a second before springing on. Then she remembered a friend who was brave and strong and plump as the moon.

'Chestnut will have the answer,' she said. She didn't like leaving the heron, all alone. But what else could she do? She patted his soft neck and emptied her pockets, placing the berries in a neat pile. They looked like a tempting treat for a daring field mouse, but if they were gone when she returned, surely Granny would understand that Damsel had to help.

She lifted, fluttering above the glittering ground, following the trail past the quiet pond with its sleeping ducks, through the golden gates, to the safety of the group of tall firs where Mummy Rabbit had her burrow. Damsel landed lightly beside some fallen cones and dashed to the mouth of the tunnel.

'Chestnut! Chestnut! Come quickly!'

After some scratching and snuffling, Chestnut appeared, munching on a leaf.

'There's a heron injured on the Doolies,' she panted. 'He's weak and needs to eat an eel.'

'Eel.' Chestnut shuddered. 'I can't swim.'

'Come on, I'll show you,' she said, as she clambered onto his back, his fur soft as moss. She gripped his floppy ears as he scampered between the trees, past the sleeping ducks, over the crunching meadow to where the heron lay.

'Gee, he's in a bad way,' said Chestnut.

'Sh! He can hear.' Damsel slid from Chestnut's back and ran around to the yellow eye so the heron could see her.

'I've brought help,' she gasped.

'Here.' Chestnut's nose twitched as he plucked tufts of down from his chest and offered it to the heron as padding.

'Thank you.' The heron's eye slid shut. 'Please ... tell Father where I am.' His voice trembled.

Damsel tried not to panic. The heronry was a long way away, up and over the forest, a place she'd never been.

The heron shivered.

'He needs to keep warm,' she said.

'Gently does it.' Chestnut's whiskers quivered as he tried to squeeze his rounded body between the heron and the ground. But it was no good. The heron was too heavy.

Damsel scrambled amongst Chestnut's fur until she was standing on his shoulder, next to the heron's eye.

'We're here,' she reassured the bird, 'but you must try.'

The heron's pulse thumped faintly beneath her fingers. Shakily, he pulled up his head until it rested on Chestnut's rump.

'Now what do we do?' Chestnut wheezed.

'I need to tell his father,' Damsel said, more bravely than she felt.

'No. It's too dangerous!'

Damsel knew Chestnut was right. Herons ate fish and frogs and snapped at baby mice and voles. A tiny fairy might look a tasty bite, particularly in the gloom. Granny wouldn't be happy if she knew what Damsel was planning. But if she didn't warn the other birds, they might drink the nasty water too. And then what would happen to Haddo?

'I won't be long,' she said, and kissed Chestnut's fluffy cheek.

But the herons nested on the opposite side of the forest. The flight was further and harder than Damsel expected. Soon her fragile wings grew tired, and she began to drop. Lower and lower and lower.

'Keep going. You can do it!' She urged herself on.

A wind gathered, blowing her right then left, up and down, as clouds shifted in front of the moon. She battled on and on, until finally, giant mounds of sticks and twigs rose out of the darkness.

She should have listened to Chestnut's warnings. She should be with Granny, cuddling in front of the fire.

But before she had time to turn back, a voice boomed from the largest nest. 'Who goes there?'

She fluttered and fluttered; her heart pounded so hard she could barely breathe.

'It's only me, Damsel the fairy,' she whimpered. 'It's about your son … He drank dirty water and now he's not well.'

Sharing her message used the last of her energy and she could flicker no more. She dropped, legs kicking, rushing towards the ground.

'Chestnut!' She screamed for her loyal friend.

Whoosh! Thwump! She landed on something feathery and strong. Her stomach lurched as she was raised high in the air again.

She rode tucked between wings, rolling like a stick in the weir.

'Tell me where he is,' the heron's father shouted.

'The Doolies!' she cried.

The heron's father flapped his powerful wings, his muscles working beneath her as they soared over the treetops, higher than she had ever flown. She saw the mansion house with its pillars, the dark islands in the centre of the lake, the fir forest where Chestnut lived, even the edge of the fairy ring that circled Granny's cottage.

The heron called. 'Kaark! Kaark! I'm telling the others to go catch eels,' he explained.

She looked ahead, searching the empty meadows, grateful for the bright moon.

'Over there. Beside the pair of pines!' She roared so her voice could be heard above the wind, clutching tightly as they dipped and swooped towards the bulky shadow.

There was a bump as the heron's feet skidded on the ground.

'Chestnut!' Damsel shouted, sliding from her feathery seat, breathless from her adventure.

'Damsel!' Chestnut twisted his head from beneath the wilted heron so he could see.

'My son!' The heron's father gently lifted the heron and wrapped him in his wings.

Chestnut shook himself.

The young heron smiled, then shut his eyes.

'Will he be okay?' Damsel held her breath.

'I'll take him back to the nest, where he can rest and eat,' the father explained. 'It's a fine thing you and your friend have done. We could never find a better home than Haddo.'

The heron's father stood, his son cradled on his back as he took a step, followed by another then another, beating his wings until they rose. They glided up and up, until Damsel was sure they were high enough to touch the stars. The father circled a 'thank you' and Damsel clapped, whilst Chestnut nibbled on the icy grass.

'Will you come with me to Granny's?' she asked, yawning, suddenly very tired. She bent and pocketed the berries, which were just as she'd left them.

Chestnut snuggled close. 'Jump on,' he said.

Climbing onto Chestnut's back took the very last of her strength, but Damsel knew she'd collected enough berries for Granny to make steaming mugs of sweet rowan juice. And best of all, the herons of Haddo were safe.

INSPIRED BY VISITORS TO HADDO

10

FOLLOW IN THE FOOTSTEPS OF ...

7th Earl of Aberdeen, Governor-General of Canada 1893-1898

Andrew Carnegie, Scottish-American Industrialist and Philanthropist

Archibald Primrose, 5th Earl of Rosebery and Prime Minister

Benjamin Britten, English Composer

Dame Esther Rantzen, Journalist & Presenter

Dame Janet Baker, Mezzo Soprano

Diana, Princess of Wales

Francois Guizot in 1858, French Politician

Fred MacAulay, Scottish Comedian

George Hamilton-Gordon, 4th Earl of Aberdeen, British Prime Minister 1852–1855

Helen Keller, American Author

Henry Morton Stanley, Politican, Author, Explorer

HRH The Duke of Edinburgh, HHCOS Royal Patron

Jackie Kay, Scottish Maker, March 2016 - March 2021

King Charles, visited as Prince Charles, Duke of Rothesay

Leon Goossens, Oboist

Magnus Magnusson, Recorded Mastermind, February 1994

Moira Stewart, British News Reader

Moody and Sankey, American Evangelists

Philip Kemble, Actor

Princess Margaret

Queen Elizabeth II

Queen Elizabeth the Queen Mother

Queen Mary of the United Kingdom (1867 – 1953), A great friend of Ishbel Gordon

Queen Victoria and Prince Albert

Ralph Vaughan Williams, Composer

Richard Douglas James Baker OBE, Broadcaster

Sheena Blackhall, Doric Makar

Tweedy the Clown, Giffords Circus

Violet Asquith, British Politician, Grandmother of actress Helena Bonham Carter

William Ewart Gladstone, Prime Minister and Writer

ACKNOWLEDGEMENTS

THANK YOU FROM US BOTH

The creation of *Haddo Reimagined* required the help of a great number of generous supporters, who offered both time and expertise. We send our heartfelt appreciation to all who helped shape our vision, with special thanks to those mentioned below.

Firstly, we thank both the Creative Aberdeenshire Network CanDo initiative, as well as Creative Scotland, for providing vital funding during the research stage of the project. *Haddo Reimagined* would not have been possible without this help.

We also extend our special appreciation to Joanna Marchioness of Aberdeen, Dr Cathy Guthrie (Operations Manager, Haddo Arts), and Libby Thomas (Arts & Events, Visitor Services Supervisor, National Trust for Scotland) for graciously allowing us to launch our book and exhibit our photographs at Haddo Arts 2024. Thank you.

The inclusion of the beautiful map of Haddo Country Park was a wish made real thanks to the generous assistance of Neil England and kind support of Haddo Arts.

In addition to our joint thanks, we also wish to show our gratitude for those who helped us individually.

THANK YOU FROM RAE COWIE

I wish to thank my good friend, writer and performer Shane Strachan, Scots Scriever 2022-23, for correcting my Doric spelling and reminding me of words I'd forgotten. All errors are my own.

Additional thanks for help with Doric go to my dear parents, Ian and Isobel Addison, who taught me how to speak the language and are still answering my questions.

Special thanks for resilience go to my Thursday writing group, Eleonora Balsano, Chris Cottom, and Barbara Marsh for bearing with some very rough drafts and helping me find the true stories within.

Many thanks to Sareen McLay for her expertise in children's writing, editing skills and assistance with the fairy tale *There Can Never Be a Better Home Than Haddo*. Also, for her patient encouragement during our many discussions about 'the Haddo project'.

Thanks also to all at the Scottish chapter of the Romantic Novelists' Association for being there when the going got tough; particular thanks to authors Mary Kingswood and Mairibeth MacMillan for fact-checking the Regency pieces and cheering me on.

A huge thank you to Susan Cunningham for both her professional proofreading skills and being a brilliant writing friend.

I would never have embarked on this project if it weren't for my husband Mark, and our sons Fraser and Malcolm, and all the happy memories of walks and time spent at Haddo Country Park. Thanks for being my constant supporters; my everything.

But my biggest thanks go to the best collaborator a writer could wish for, Susan Orr, who completed the initial legwork, whilst my leg healed! Her curiosity and love of the natural world has inspired a stunning photographic collection, which helped me discover things anew at Haddo. I'm immensely grateful for her unwavering belief in *Haddo Reimagined* and her determination to publish our work. I look forward with interest to what she does next

THANK YOU FROM SUSAN ORR

I wish to offer thanks to Suzanna Atkinson (former Haddo Visitor Services Officer), Laurie Malster (Haddo Assistant Visitor Services Officer), John Malster (Ecologist), and the Friends of Haddo Country Park volunteers, who have dedicated time and effort into maintaining the charm and beauty of this special park.

Thanks are extended to the volunteers at the Tarves Heritage Project, in particular Moira Minty and Danny Paterson, for their assistance during my research phase, and to Vivien Gauld for generously granting permission to use the photograph of Haddo Pheasantry, a place with personal significance in Vivien's family history.

Special thanks to Paul Nicol, not only a talented photographer but also a good friend, who generously gave his time to provide invaluable editing advice for my project images.

Huge thanks to Claire, Louise, Eva, Patrick, and Isabella, for your support and friendship throughout this project. My sister Claire has a great eye for detail and provided helpful, honest feedback during my first edits. Thank you to my dear friend Louise for our countless walks around Haddo Country Park, rain or shine, and for always showing interest in the project's progress. Eva's photography skills and advice were much appreciated. Exploring Haddo, especially in the sensory garden with Patrick and Isabella, was delightful. Capturing a moment of Patrick looking through Ray Shaw's memorial camera was a highlight.

Heartfelt thanks to my husband, Gordon, and our sons, James and Adam, for consistently offering their 'creative input' throughout the evolution of *Haddo Reimagined*.

Lastly, gratitude to Rae, my creative partner, for inviting me to collaborate on this wonderful project. Working alongside you has been an absolute pleasure, and I have learnt so much. Your writing talent is remarkable, and the stories you create are nothing short of amazing. Turning our vision into reality by creating our *Haddo Reimagined* book and presenting it at the Haddo Arts Festival is a dream realised.

Hygrocybe Punicea

Astrantia

Rae Cowie writes short fiction with pieces published by the Scottish Field magazine, Splonk, Bath Award, Oxford Flash Prize, Postbox Magazine, Northwords Now, Aberdeen University Elphinstone Institute and more.

In 2022, she was thrilled to be granted a prestigious Scottish Book Trust Award.

Another writing highlight came when her piece *The Fight of the Wyld Cattis* was included in the Great Scottish Canvas, published by the WWF Scotland, issued to delegates attending the UN Climate Change Conference in Glasgow.

In 2015, she won the esteemed Romantic Novelists' Association Elizabeth Goudge Award.
Rae is currently submitting a new short fiction collection to editors. Discover more about her work at
www.raecowie.com

Susan Orr is a graduate of Gray's School of Art with a BA in Photography. Her projects investigate the deep-rooted connection humans hold with the natural world. Her work aims to spark curiosity with nature and the history that surrounds us.

Susan was a winner in the Aberdeen Harbour Board Photography Competition 2019. The Winners' exhibition is on display in Aberdeen International Airport.

In 2022, Susan was awarded a grant from the Aberdeenshire Creative Network to collaborate with a published author and deliver phase 1 of a new photography project.

Susan's website can be found at
www.susanorrart.com

Papaver Orientale Bud

GLOSSARY OF DORIC TERMS

DORIC TERMS INCLUDED IN BRICK BY BRICK (PAGE16)

Aa – all

Ablow – below

Aff – off

Ain – own

Althou – although

Ane – one

Anither – another

Ay – yes

Aye – always

Bairn – child

Baith – both

Bannock – oatcake

Bather – bother

Beets – boots

Biden – dwelling

Biggin – building

Bourach – group/pile

Chooks – hens

Claik – gossip

Cloot – cloth

Cooshie doos – wood pigeons

Daunderin – strolling

Doos – pigeons

Drappit – dropped

Dreels – drills, small furrows for sowing seed

Dryin ropes – clothes lines

Een – eye/eyes

Fa – who

Fainted clean awa – passed out

Fair – really

Faither – father

Fan – when

Fantoosh – grand/ fancy

Far – where

Feart – afraid

Firie – fire

Fit – what

Fit wye – why

Flee – fly

Freen – friend

Gairden – garden

Gan – going

Gey – rather/ somewhat

Ging – go

Girdle – Griddle

Gweed-mither – mother-in-law

Hairst – harvest

Hame – home

Han – help

Heid – head

Kennin – knowing

Kent – knew

Kirk – church

Lang – long

Lavvie – toilet

Loon – lad/boy

Mair – more

Maist – most

Muckle – large

Nae – not

Neep – turnip

Nib – nose

Noo – now

O – of

Oors – ours

Oot – out

Ower – over

Peelie-wally – pale/ sickly

Phasies – pheasants

Pit – put

Pucklie – a small amount

Reid – red

Saa – saw

Scrappit – scrapped

Sharn – dung/dirt

Si – so

Skiff – to move in a light and airy manner

Summin – something

Reef – roof

Tattieboodie – scarecrow

Thocht – thought

Thrapple – throat

Trickit – delighted

Tyauve – work strenuously/ struggle

Weel – well

Wi – with

Wid – would

Wis – was

Won him roun – won him round

Wunnert – wondered

DORIC TERMS INCLUDED IN BUTTERBUR (PAGE 38)

A – a or an

Aboot – about

Aifter – after

Ain – own

An – and

Auld – old

Aye – always

Bile – boil

Claik – gossip

Deen – done

Div – do

Fan – when

Fit – what

Gaup – gape

Hae – have

Hairm – harm

Hame – home

Haud your wheest – be quiet

Heid – head

Ma – my

Mine – remember

Mither – mother

Nae – no or not

O – of

Peer – poor

Quine – a girl

Reets – roots

Sair heids – headaches

Snecked – latched

Spik – speak

Sproots – sprouts

Stanes – stones

Wi – with

Wid – would

Wifie – woman/ wife

Yersel – yourself

Milton Keynes UK
Ingram Content Group UK Ltd.
UKHW051812290824
447587UK00002B/17